When Grandma Came

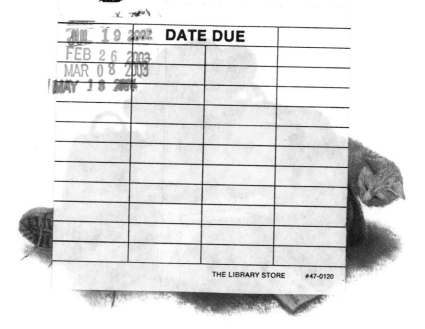

Written by Jill Paton Walsh

ILLUSTRATED BY SOPHY WILLIAMS

PUFFIN BOOKS

When Grandma came to stay she said to Madeleine...

"I have been to Mount Desert Island, far away,

and seen the shape of a great whale rolling in the deep...

...but I have never, no never,
seen anything as tremendous as you!

I have been to the Arctic ice-plains, far away,

and watched the polar bear amble and gambol at midnight...

...but I have never, no never,
known anything as wakeful as you!

I have been to the lake shores of Africa, far away,

and seen the great hippopotamus roll in the mud-banks...

...but I have never, no never,
seen anything as messy as you!

I have been to the bush in Australia, far away,

and met the kangaroo bounding across the grasslands...

...but I have never, no never,
met anything as bouncy as you!

I have been to the jungles of India, far away,

and heard the tiger roar in the stripy shadows...

...but I have never, no never,
heard anything as rowdy as you!

I have sailed on the great Nile river, far away,

and seen how the land grows green between desert and desert...

...but I have never, no never,
known anything growing like you!

I remember moonlight and starlight on valleys and mountains

and seas and cities and gardens the wide world over...

...but I never remember anything as heaven-and-earthly as you!"

"I love you too, Grandma," said Madeleine.